LET'S GO ON AN ADVENTURE!

Copyright © 2020
Aunt Mels BookNook

LET'S LEARN ABOUT AUSTRALIA

Barking Owl
They bark like a dog.
Crikey!

Magpie
They lay 16 eggs
at once.

Rainbow Finch
They eat up to 1/3 of
their weight each day.

Blue-Winged Kookaburra
They make an OW
sound, like WOW!

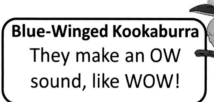

Little (Fairy) Penguin
They are the smallest
penguin, only 13" high.
And they really are blue!

Lyrebird
They can make their
voice sound like a
Koala and a Dingo.

Ibis
They dig in the mud to find
food, they like crayfish.

Laughing Kookaburra
They laugh like people.

Cassowary
Australia's heaviest bird, it
weighs about 100 pounds.

Indigenous Peoples

Indigenous Peoples are also known as First People. They are the earliest known people to live in Australia, and have the oldest continuous culture on the planet. There are still Indigenous Peoples living in Australia. Their art is the longest continuing art form in history. They invented the Digeridoo, which is a wooden, wind instrument, it's the oldest instrument ever. They also invented the Boomerang. The Boomerang is the first "heavier than air" machine made by humans. Boomerangs are fun, but Arhat prefers a Frisbee for his favorite "heavier than air" flying machine.

Arhat

Blue-Tongued Skink Lizard

This is Australia's Blue-Tongued Skink. It lives in the grasslands, or even in your gardens. They are great to have in a garden because they eat garden pests. When they feel threatened they will hiss ant stick out their long blue tongue. They grow to be about 2 feet long, and can live for 30 years.

FUN FACT: They lay babies, not eggs, and can lay 20 babies at one time.

Echidna

This is Australia's adorable Echidna.
These cute creatures are rarely seen
because they burrow into the ground
and live there.
They weigh between 5 to 20 pounds.
Their tongue is 7 inches long, they
use it to eat insects and worms.

FUN FACT: Their babies are called
Puggles.

Emu

The Emu is Australia's tallest bird. They grow to about 6 ½ feet tall and weigh on average about 80 pounds. Despite their huge size they eat only leaves, grasshoppers and beetles.
One Emu egg can feed 4 to 6 adults.

FUN FACT: They have two sets of eyelids. One is for blinking, the other keeps out dust.

Red Kangaroo

The Kangaroo is the tallest of all plant eating marsupials.
A marsupial is an animal that carry their babies in a pouch.
Kangaroos can jump 6 feet high, and jump a length of 29 feet.
They live to be over 20 years old.

FUN FACT: They can go a long time without drinking water.
They get all the water they need from the leaves
they eat.

Koala

This is Australia's beloved Koala. A Koala is not a bear, it is a marsupial, just like the Kangaroo. They are about 25 to 30 inches tall, and weigh between 10 to 30 pounds. They eat eucalyptus leaves for up to 20 hours a day.

FUN FACT: Koalas eat so many eucalyptus leaves, a Koala can smell like a cough drop.

Numbat

The Numbat is a very small marsupial. They grow to be about 15 to 18 inches tall. Their tongue is about 4 inches long and very sticky. They use their tongue to catch termites, which is all they eat.

FUN FACT: In addition to their long tongue, the Numbat has 52 teeth. That's a lot of teeth brushing!

Quokka

The Quokka is a small marsupial, about 16 inches tall. They are nocturnal, which means they sleep during the day and stay awake at night. They look like they are always smiling, but they can actually be quite aggressive.

FUN FACT: They can be mischievous and like to break into people's houses at night and eat their food.

Quoll

The adorable Quoll can grow to be between 30 to 50 inches long.
They weigh between 2 to 8 pounds.
They eat anything from insects to chickens.

FUN FACT: Their babies are called pups, and when they're born they are the size of a grain a rice.

Tasmanian Devil

The Tasmanian Devil is very small, but very strong. They weigh about 30 pounds. They travel about 10 miles a day. They have the most powerful bite of any Australian animal. They eat birds, fish and snakes.

FUN FACT: When they get scared they make a horrible scream, and that's how they got their name.

Wombat

The adorable Wombat is quite round. Wombats can be very friendly to people. They are about 3 feet tall, and can weigh up to 75 pounds. Despite their short legs they can run about 25 miles an hour.

FUN FACT: A Wombat has very strong claws, they can dig through tree roots.

Dingo

The Australian Dingo is a wild dog. They weigh around 25 to 45 pounds. They do not bark, but howl like a wolf. Dingoes are very intelligent, and very good hunters. Sometimes Dingoes will eat animals as big as sheep. To stop Dingoes from eating sheep Australia built the biggest fence ever. That fence is over 5,000 feet long.

FUN FACT: Dingoes have rotating wrists, because of this they can open doors, just like people can.

Crocodile

This is Australia's salt water Crocodile. Australian's call them Salties. Crocodiles can live up to 70 years. Crocodiles weigh between 1,000 to 2,000 pounds. They are excellent swimmers, and can go as fast as 15 miles per hour.

FUN FACT: They will kill very large prey, like water buffalo and sharks.

But, before we go
A few questions for you...

Which was your favorite animal?

Who was the silliest animal?

Who was the scariest animal?

Which animal do you want as a pet?

What was the best fun fact?

What was your favorite thing about the Indigenous Peoples?

Which do you prefer, Boomerang or Frisbee?

Thank you for coming on our adventure with us! We hope you had as much fun as much as we did. We loved learning about all of the cool animals. And we especially loved that you joined us on our trip to wild, wonderful Australia!

Catch You Later Mates!

Made in the USA
Middletown, DE
11 November 2023

42432477R00022